It's Fun to Draw
Princesses
and
Ballerinas

Mark Bergin

WINDMILL
BOOKS
New York

Published in 2012 by Windmill Books, LLC
303 Park Avenue South, Suite #1280, New York, NY 10010-3657

Editor: Rob Walker
U.S. Editor: Sara Antill

Library of Congress Cataloging-in-Publication Data

Bergin, Mark.
 Princesses and ballerinas / by Mark Bergin. — 1st ed.
     p. cm. — (It's fun to draw)
 Includes index.
 ISBN 978-1-61533-351-6 (library binding)
 1. Princesses in art—Juvenile literature. 2. Ballet dancers in art—Juvenile literature. 3. Drawing—Technique—Juvenile literature. I. Title.
 NC825.P75B47 2012
 743.4'4—dc22

                            2010052107

Manufactured in Heshan, China

CPSIA Compliance Information: Batch #SS1102WM:
For Further Information contact Windmill Books, New York,
New York at 1-866-478-0556

Contents

Princess Anna

1 Start with the head. Add a nose, a mouth, and dots for eyes.

2 Add the arms and the dress's top.

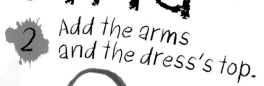

3 Draw the hair and crown.

Splat-a-Fact!
Princesses often live in castles.

You Can Do It!
Use a felt-tip pen for the lines and add color using colored pencils. Use the pencils in a scribbly way to add texture.

3 Add the dress and the feet.

Louise

1 Start with the head. Add a face.

2 Add the hair and an ear.

You Can Do It!

Use a brown felt-tip pen for the lines and add color with pencils.

3 Draw the dress.

Splat-a-Fact!

Ballerinas have to work hard and practice every day.

4 Add the arms and legs.

5 Add dress details and a bow.

Henrietta

 1 Start with the head. Add a nose, a mouth, and dots for eyes.

 2 Add the hair.

3 Draw the top of the tutu and a big circle for the skirt.

You Can Do It!

Use crayons for all textures and paint over your picture with watercolor paint. Use a blue felt-tip pen for the lines.

4 Add the legs.

5 Draw the arms.

Splat-a-Fact!

Ballerinas can wear out two to three pairs of ballet shoes in one week.

9

Princess Margot

1 Start with the head. Add the nose, mouth, and dots for the eyes.

3 Draw the arms and the feet.

You Can Do It!

Use wax crayons for all textures and paint over your picture with colored inks.

2 Add the dress.

4 Add the crown and the hair.

5 Draw the details of the dress.

10

Splat-a-Fact!
In one famous story, a princess befriends a frog. In the end, the frog turns into a prince when she kisses him!

11

Princess Lisa

1 Draw a circle for the head. Add a nose, a mouth, and dots for eyes.

2 Add hair and a crown.

3 Draw the top of the dress.

Splat-a-Fact!
In some stories, princesses have a different dress for each day of the year.

You Can Do It!
Use crayons to add texture. Then paint over your drawing with watercolors.

4 Add the arms and a purse shaped like a heart.

5 Draw the dress and feet.

Marina

1 Cut out the head and glue it down. Draw a mouth and a dot for the eye.

2 Cut out the top of the tutu and glue it down. Cut out the shape of the skirt and glue it down.

You Can Do It!

Start with a piece of colored paper for the background. Cut out shapes for the spotlight and floor. Glue them down. Now cut out all the shapes for the ballerina and glue them down in the order shown.

3 Cut out the legs and feet. Glue the legs down first, then add shoes.

4 Cut out the hair and glue it down. Cut out the arms and glue them down.

Make sure you get an adult to help you when using scissors!

splat-a-Fact!
A tutu can take
about 60 to 70 hours
to make.

Princess Helena

 1 Start with the head. Add a mouth and a dot for the eye.

 **2** Add the hair and crown.

 **3** Draw three circles for the top of the dress.

Splat-a-Fact!
Princesses appear in fairy tales from all around the world.

 **4** Add the arms.

You Can Do It!
Use wax crayons for the color and a blue felt-tip pen for the lines.

 **5** Draw the dress and feet.

17

Princess Melissa

1

Draw a circle for the head. Add a nose, a mouth, and dots for eyes.

2 Draw the dress.

3 Add the arms.

Splat-a-Fact!
British royal Princess Anne competed in the 1976 Olympics.

You Can Do It!
Use a soft pencil for the lines and add color using watercolor paint.

4

Draw the ropes and the swing. Add the feet.

5 Add the hair and crown.

19

Jennifer

1 Start with a head. Add a nose, a mouth, and dots for eyes.

2 Add the hair.

3 Draw the dress.

you Can Do It!

Add color using colored pencils. Use a black felt-tip pen for the lines, the shoes, and the pattern on the tutu.

4 Add the arms and legs.

5 Color in the dress and shoes.

splat-a-Fact!

Ballerinas need to have strong ankles and knees.

Princess Nicole

 1

Draw a circle for the head. Add a face.

2 Draw the top of the dress.

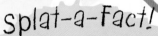

3

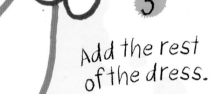

Add the rest of the dress.

You Can Do It!

Use a felt-tip pen for the lines.
Add color using colored pencils.
Use the pencils in a scribbly
way to add interest.

Splat-a-Fact!

Hans Christian Andersen
wrote "The Princess and
the Pea."

4

Add the arms
and feet.

5

Draw the hair
and crown.

Princess Heather

1 Start with the head. Add a nose, a mouth, and dots for eyes.

2 Add the hair.

3 Add the hat and veil.

you Can Do It!
Use a green felt-tip pen for the lines and add color using watercolor paint.

Splat-a-Fact!
Movie star Grace Kelly became a princess when she married the prince of Monaco.

5 Add the skirt and the feet.

4 Draw the arms and sleeves.

Amanda

1 Draw a circle for the head. Add a nose, a mouth, and dots for eyes.

2 Add the hair and ears.

3 Draw the tutu.

You Can Do It!

Use a purple felt-tip pen for the lines and add color using colored inks.

4 Add the arms and legs.

Splat-a-Fact!

Dancing *en pointe* is performed by standing on the tips of your toes.

5 Finish drawing details.

27

Kirsten

1 Draw an oval for the head. Add a nose, a mouth, and dots for eyes.

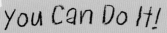

You Can Do It!

Use a purple felt-tip pen for the lines and add color with soft, chalky pastels. Smudge and blend some of the colors to add interest.

2 Add the hair.

3 Draw the tutu.

Splat-a-Fact!

"Pas de deux" means "a dance for two."

4 Add the arms and legs.

5 Finish the details of the dress. Add a hairband.

Fiona

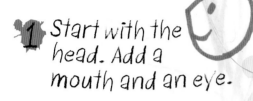 **1** Start with the head. Add a mouth and an eye.

 **2** Add the hair.

 **3** Draw the tutu.

You Can Do It!

Use wax crayons to add color and a blue felt-tip pen for lines. Smudge or blend the color for more interest.

 **4** Add the legs.

5 Draw the arms.

Splat-a-Fact!

It can take over 100 yards (91 m) of tulle to make a tutu.

Read More

Castle, Kate. *My First Ballet Book*. London: Kingfisher, 2011.

Levy, Barbara Soloff. *How to Draw Princesses and Other Fairy Tale Pictures*. Mineola, NY: Dover Publications, 2008.

Wilding, Valerie. *Real Princesses: An Inside Look at Royal Life*. New York: Walker Books for Young Readers, 2007.

Glossary

pastel (pa-STEL) A kind of chalklike crayon used in drawing.

smudge (SMUJ) To blend together

texture (TEKS-chur) How something feels when you touch it.

tulle (TOOL) A thin, sheer fabric.

tutu (TOO-too) A short skirt worn by ballerinas.

watercolor (WAH-ter-kuh-ler) A paint made by mixing color and water.

Index

Web Sites

For Web resources related to the subject of this book,
go to: www.windmillbooks.com/weblinks and select this book's title.